Put Beginning Readers on the Right Track with
ALL ABOARD READING™

The All Aboard Reading series is especially for beginning readers. Written by noted authors and illustrated in full color, these are books that children really and truly *want* to read—books to excite their imagination, tickle their funny bone, expand their interests, and support their feelings. With five different reading levels, All Aboard Reading lets you choose which books are most appropriate for your children and their growing abilities.

Picture Readers—for Ages 3 to 6
Picture Readers have super-simple texts, with many nouns appearing as rebus pictures. At the end of each book are 24 flash cards—on one side is the rebus picture; on the other side is the written-out word.

Pre-Level 1—for Ages 4 to 6
First Friends, First Readers have a super-simple text starring lovable recurring characters. Each book features two easy stories that will hold the attention of even the youngest reader while promoting an early sense of accomplishment.

Level 1—for Preschool through First-Grade Children
Level 1 books have very few lines per page, very large type, easy words, lots of repetition, and pictures with visual "cues" to help children figure out the words on the page.

Level 2—for First-Grade to Third-Grade Children
Level 2 books are printed in slightly smaller type than Level 1 books. The stories are more complex, but there is still lots of repetition in the text, and many pictures. The sentences are quite simple and are broken up into short lines to make reading easier.

Level 3—for Second-Grade through Third-Grade Children
Level 3 books have considerably longer texts, harder words, and more complicated sentences.

All Aboard for happy reading!

D0710122

For my sister, Karen
(almost-author of *Ugly Glasses*)—K.C.

For my husband, Bob, with love—H.H.M.

Library of Congress Cataloging-in-Publication Data

Cristaldi, Kathryn.
   Princess Lulu goes to camp / by Kathryn Cristaldi ; illustrated by
Heather Harms Maione.
      p.   cm. — (All aboard reading. Level 2)
   Summary: Princess Lulu has no friends because she is "a royal pain" so the king and
queen send her to Camp Ruff 'n' Tuff where they hope she will learn to get along.
   [1. Princesses—Fiction. 2. Camps—Fiction. 3. Friendship—Fiction.] I. Maione,
Heather Harms, ill. II. Title.
III. Series.
PZ7.C86964Pr 1997
[E]—dc20

96-30742
CIP
AC

ISBN 0-448-41125-3   E F G H I J

ALL
ABOARD
READING™
Level 2
Grades 1-3

Princess Lulu
Goes to Camp

By Kathryn Cristaldi
Illustrated by Heather Harms Maione

Grosset & Dunlap • New York

Lulu was a princess.

She lived in a big castle near a big lake
with a big fountain in the middle.

People came from all over
to see the castle.

They came to see Lulu's father,
the king,
and Lulu's mother, the queen.

Sometimes they even came
to see Lulu.

"No autographs, please,"

Lulu would say with a sniff.

Then she would wave a little wave,

and nod a little nod,

and turn to her right.

That was her best side.

Everyone said so.

Life in the castle was fun.

Lulu had her own

princess-sized bedroom.

It had a princess-sized water bed,

a princess-sized TV,

and a pale pink princess telephone.

"No princess should be without one,"

she would say to herself.

"It's too cold!"

Lulu would screech into the phone.

Then a maid would race up

with a fuzzy pink blanket.

"Snack!" she would scream
at the top of her lungs.
Then a chef would rush in
with a plate of cookies.

Anything Lulu wanted, Lulu had.

But there was one thing

Lulu did not have.

She did not have a friend.

"Who needs them!"

she would say

to a spot on her wall.

But the king and queen were worried.

They spoke to the royal wise man.

"She's smart," said the king.

"She's pretty," said the queen.

The wise man put one arm

around the king,

and one arm around the queen.

"She's a royal pain!" he said.

"Oh, my!" said the queen.

"Oh, dear!" said the king.

But they knew he was right.

"She must learn to get along
with others," said the wise man.
"Perhaps a summer camp would help.
I suggest Camp Ruff 'n' Tuff."
He showed them a booklet.

All the campers
have to make
their own beds.

All the campers
have to learn
to make a fire.

"Ew!" said the queen.

"Ugh!" said the king.

But they knew he was right.

The next day the princess got on

a big yellow bus.

It smelled like Twizzle sticks

and oranges and tuna fish.

"My stars!" said Lulu,

holding her nose.

"No, my <u>lunch</u>,"

said the girl sitting next to her.

"Want some?"

Lulu stared straight ahead.

"I guess not," said the girl.

Then she stuck her head

out the window and yelled,

"Camp Ruff 'n' Tuff,

here we come!"

Camp Ruff 'n' Tuff had five bunks,
a mess hall, and a tiny lake.
"No yacht?" asked Lulu.
Then she waited for someone
to carry her bags.

18

"Do you need a hand?"

said the girl with the tuna sandwich.

"We are in the same bunk."

Lulu rolled her eyes.

But she handed over her bags.

"You're welcome," said the girl.

Bunk C had four bunk beds,

two light bulbs,

and one counselor—

Janine.

"Listen up," said Janine.

"There will be no gum chewing,

no messy beds, and no talking

after lights-out."

The girl with the tuna sandwich
made a face.

"She forgot no <u>fun</u>," she whispered.

"No <u>phone</u>?!" screeched Lulu.

Then she looked on the shelves
and under the beds.
"No TV, either!" She gulped.

The next morning Lulu screamed

for her breakfast, but no one came.

So she put on her best dress

and her best shoes

and her best sparkly crown.

Then she walked to the mess hall.

On the way, three things happened.

First she got stung
by a bee.

Then she fell
in the mud.

Then her crown landed in the lake.

"Look, it's a mud monster!"

said the tuna sandwich girl

when she saw Lulu.

She pulled Lulu's shoe

out of the mud.

And fished her crown out of the lake.

She even loaned Lulu

her favorite Squid Man T-shirt.

"You're welcome," said Tuna.

Lulu fixed her crown.

"I am not a happy camper,"

she said.

Tuna giggled.

"You are funny," she said.

Then she giggled some more.

Lulu smiled.

A teeny tiny smile.

She had never made anyone

giggle before.

"Bunk C, report to the lake!"

said a voice over the loudspeaker.

"That's us," said Tuna.

They ran to their bunk and

put on their swimsuits.

Lulu pulled on

her royal bathing cap.

"Nice cap," said Tuna.

Lulu patted her head.

"You're welcome," said Tuna.

At the lake,

kids were laughing and splashing.

Tuna jumped off the dock.

"Come on in!" she yelled.

Lulu stuck one toe in the water.

"It's too cold," she said.

Lulu watched everyone

laughing and splashing.

It looked like fun.

She closed her eyes and jumped.

"HELP!" screamed Lulu,

when she hit the water.

Tuna swam over.

"What's wrong?" she asked.

Lulu waved her arms in the air.

"I forgot," she choked.

"I can't swim."

Tuna giggled.

"Try standing," she said.

"Oh," said Lulu.

She stopped waving her arms.

"HAW! HAW! HAW!"

laughed Tuna.

"You are <u>so</u> funny!"

Lulu giggled a teeny tiny giggle.

"I am funny," she said to herself.

On Friday,

Bunk C went on an overnight.

They marched for five miles.

"Move it! Move it!"

barked Janine.

They pitched tents.

They chopped wood for a campfire.

For dinner they cooked hot dogs
over the fire.
All of a sudden,
everyone started screaming.

They were pointing at Tuna.

"Skunk! Right behind you!"

yelled a girl with a blonde ponytail.

"Run for your life!"

screamed someone else.

"Major stink bomb!"

shouted a girl with purple sneakers.

"Every camper for herself!" yelled Janine.

She dove behind a tree.

Soon everyone was hiding.

Except for Tuna.

She was too scared to move.

"Help!" she squeaked.

Lulu stood up.

She marched over to the skunk.

"Skunk, begone!" she ordered

in her loudest princess voice.

She stamped her foot on the ground.

She shook her royal crown in the air.

"Begone, I say!"

The skunk took

one look at Lulu

and raced off into the woods.

Everyone clapped and cheered.

Tuna giggled.

"You are a real friend,"

she said to Lulu.

"Thanks for helping me out."

Lulu smiled a teeny tiny smile.

"You're welcome," Lulu said.

After that, the princess and Tuna
did everything together.

They told stories after lights-out.

They made friendship bracelets
in arts and crafts.

Lulu even learned how to swim
(well, sort of).

Then it was time to go home.

On the bus,

Tuna gave Lulu a present.

It was a pencil with her address on it.

"Now we can be pencil pals," she said.

The next day,

Lulu sat on her princess-sized bed.

She thought about Camp Ruff 'n' Tuff.

Then she wrote a letter—

a letter to her new friend.

"No princess should be without one,"

she said to herself.

And she smiled

a great, big princess-sized smile.